Angels O₁

Naha.

Iris Watts

Illustrated by
Jo Dowers & Molly Moore

COUNTRY BOOKS

Dedication

To my grandson, Alex

Text © 2016 Iris Watts
Illustrations © 2106 Jo Dowers & Molly Moore
No part of this publication may be used without permission.

British Library Cataloguing-in-Publication Data.
A catalogue for this book is available from the British Library.

ISBN 978-1-910489-39-0

Published by Country Books
Courtyard Cottage, Little Longstone, Bakewell, Derbyshire DE45 1NN
Tel: 01629 640670: Email: dickrichardson@country-books.co.uk
Websites: www.countrybooks.biz
        www.sussexbooks.co.uk

Printed by 4edge Ltd., 7aEldon Way, Hockley, Essex SS5 4AD

Contents

The Assembly

Stevie never liked these grand occasions. He always felt silly and stupid although his friend, Angelina, had told him he looked fine in his big, sparkly glasses. She'd even polished his wings for him and smoothed down his yellow hair which would stick up like the bristles on a hedgehog. He'd almost forgotten his halo but Angelina had glared at him and pointed to her own shining circle around her head.

'Come on, Stevie, pull yourself together. You know Michael likes us to be on time.'

So there he was, little Stevie, friend of children, sitting cross-legged on a cloud along with thousands of other angels, staring up at the great Michael, the beloved of The Holy One, and the slayer of dragons.

Michael looked his usual glorious self, tall and commanding, with his big wings folded neatly away, his face shining with love for The Holy One whom he had served loyally ever since The Beginning.

Sitting next to Michael were two other big angels, Gabriel and Raphael – Gabriel with his beautiful face, full of love for all human beings even if they were very bad indeed. Stevie loved Gabriel. He thought him the greatest of all the Big Wings, (that was what he called the Archangels, the most important angels.) Raphael was the clever one, always thinking about the best way to do things, but Gabriel was the one who loved best and was always happy to help you.

There were some bad angels, too, of course. But more of them later!!

At a sign from Gabriel, the musical angels, sitting together on their own cloud, stopped playing the sweet

music and carefully laid down their harps and pipes and drums next to them. When all was quiet, Michael stood up and surveyed the vast assembly of angels.

He looked a rather scary figure, Stevie thought, with his stern face and eyes flashing sparks of fire. Stevie felt sure he was looking at him and tried to crouch down as low as he could so that Michael shouldn't be able to see him.

'My beloved friends,' said Michael, his clear voice carrying to the ranks of angels sitting on the furthest cloud. The Holy One has asked me to call this meeting so that I can give everyone his message.

First of all, he wants me to thank you for all your hard work, especially you, the guardian angels of children,' he said, looking straight at Stevie.

'You have saved so many children from being sad and worried, but things are getting very hard for the humans on our planet, Earth. There are many more children without fathers and mothers, many more children feeling cold and hungry and lonely. Our enemy, the wicked Malus Maximus, is becoming more and more expert in hurting children. He has got his own pack of bad angels who tell children to do bad things. Some of them even dress up as good angels, like us.'

Stevie nodded in agreement. He knew all about Malus Maximus, whom he called Old Maxie, and knew that his followers could do a lot of damage. He felt his halo, which was a bit on the big side, slip down onto his forehead, bumping into his sparkly glasses and he hastily pushed his glasses back onto his nose. Angelina glared at him and wriggled closer to him.

'Shh!…Keep still! This cloud is not big enough for us if you fidget all the time. Now look at what you've done.

Michael has noticed us and he's going to tell us off. Why do you always cause trouble?'

Michael had indeed seen Stevie. He stopped talking and glared across at Stevie.

'You again, Stephen! (People always called him Stephen when they were cross with him) Can't you keep still for just a short time? You must show respect for Raphael and Gabriel and myself. In showing respect for us you show respect for The Holy One. If you don't stop fidgeting, I shall have to banish you to one of the furthest clouds.'

All the other angels turned to look at him and he heard some of them begin to snigger. He felt hot with embarrassment and looked down at his feet, cross-legged on the cloud. 'Why did these things always have to happen to him?' he thought. 'Why did he have to wear these stupid glasses, even though they were very smart and suited him? Or so his friends said.'

Then he saw kind Gabriel whisper some-thing to Michael who nodded and looked again at Stevie, this time with a kinder expression on his face.

'So, Stephen, Gabriel tells me that you have been a very hard worker and have made a lot of children happy. The Holy One also thinks highly of you, so you are forgiven for now. But do try to listen carefully and sit still, otherwise you will fall off that cloud and get mixed up with the astronauts who are wandering around space at the moment.'

The angels smiled politely and Angelina looked approvingly at Stevie. He breathed a sigh of relief and tried to concentrate on what Michael was saying. He went on talking about all the children who were having a hard time on Earth – ('As if he knew anything about them,' thought Stevie rebelliously. These Big Wings sit around all day, drinking delicious drinks and eating heavenly bread dipped in honey and think up things for us to do.')

'Now you, Stephen,' said Michael suddenly, nearly making Stevie fall off his cloud in fright. Tell us where you work on Earth. What is your particular patch these days? Stand up when you're spoken to.'

It was difficult to stand up on a very small cloud, but Angelina held on tightly to the bottom of his tunic and stopped him from wobbling.

'In Sussex, Sir. I work with Angelina and Benedicta and Mick, Victor and Pat. We do our best. Sir.'

Then we shall be keeping an eye on you,' said Michael with a twinkle in his eye. 'Work hard and save the children from getting into trouble. If we are to defeat Malus, we have to be on the alert all the time.'

Stevie couldn't keep silent, however hard he tried. 'But Sir,' he stammered, Ignoring Angelina who was trying to make him sit down.

'We do try very hard to make our children happy. But please, what do you do, and all the other senior angels? Whilst we are on call all day and night and don't get much time off, where are you?'

A sigh, like the rustle of the wind in the long grass, rippled round the Assembly and all the angels turned to look at Stevie again. What would Michael do? Shout at Stevie and order his own security angels to haul Stevie away to one of the furthest clouds? Would Michael cancel all his duties as a guardian angel and order him out of the Heavenly kingdom?

But Michael knew Stevie meant well and really wanted to know how things worked.

'Stephen, we try to save the whole world which The Holy One created for everyone to enjoy and be happy. We continuously fight the great enemy, Malus. You save the children and we try to save the planet Earth. Remember that. Now that is all I want to say. Go away and do your duty and bring some happiness to the children of this sad planet Earth.'

Then spreading wide his mighty wings and signally to Raphael and Gabriel to follow him, Michael flew away.

Stevie looked at his friends.

'Well, we know what we have to do. Save the children. That's what Big Wings wants us to do. So, we'd better get going.'

"Don't Be Afraid"

Four days to go! Four days until the end of term. And then it would be Christmas. It was, thought Josh, (whose real name was Joshua, but all his friends called him Josh,) the very best time of the year. They had already decorated the classroom with paintings of reindeer and snow men and Father Christmas; and the tree, standing in the entrance hall, looked wonderful with all its coloured balls and stars especially when Mr Livingstone, the headmaster, turned on the lights. That afternoon, the children were going over to the church to see the Crib and to sing some special Christmas songs which were called carols.

Josh was making Christmas cards which were to be sold at the school fair on the last day of term, and he was trying to write Happy Christmas like the monks used to do, with the capital letters decorated with birds and flowers. He finished the one he was making and stuck a big yellow star on the front of the card and gave a sigh of happiness. He was small for his age, he was seven, but was always cheerful and his class mates liked him. He had a small face with bright brown eyes and short brown hair and he could run very fast in the races at Sports Day at the end of term. His brother Paul teased him, though, and he didn't like that. Paul was in the top class and was going to the Big School next September, whilst Josh loved his little village school with its kind teachers who knew everybody and didn't boss everyone around.

As he made a neat pile of all the finished Christmas cards, he hummed one of the Christmas songs they were going to sing that afternoon in the church. It was called "Away in a manger" and Josh liked this song best of all. Josh was in the school choir and because he was small, he stood in the front row and everyone looked at him and he didn't mind at all. His brother, Paul called him a Show Off and said he sang like one of Gran's chickens when you chased it round its pen.

In fact, Josh had a beautiful voice – like an angel's voice, said his teacher, Mrs Browning. It was a sweet, high voice that rang out as clear as a bell. So Josh ignored his brother and told him he looked stupid in his new football shorts which were too big for him as their mother said Paul was growing so fast that she didn't want to buy him any more shorts for two years.

That afternoon, the children went over to the church for a rehearsal. The village of Maryfield, where Josh lived, was lucky to have a village school, which had been there for ages and ages, and only had a hundred pupils. The village also had a very old church where, a long time ago, some holy men, known as monks, lived and worked and said their prayers.

It was warm and peaceful in the church and the afternoon winter sun was streaming through the west window with all its coloured glass casting patterns of light on the floor. Mrs Browning showed them the model of Mary and Joseph and the child Jesus which had been put in the side chapel and told them that the school was going to perform its own Nativity play for all the parents to see and the choir was going to sing some carols.

As the children took their seats in the main part of the church, Josh was told to stand out front with the choir as they would all be singing as soon as the performers were ready to start.

The school was lucky to have Jasmin in the top class who was to play the part of Mary. Her family had come to England from the land where Jesus was born and grew up, and she looked perfect for the part in her long dress and blue cloak. The boy who played Joseph lived in the village where his father was the blacksmith and he, too, was in the top class. Two of the Wise Men came from over-seas and their families had settled in the village.

Jacob came from Syria and Ben's family came from China. The third wise man, Tony, came from the village next to Maryfield. They were all dressed up in Eastern clothes and they looked very fine indeed.

As they took up their positions in the front part of the church, the Headmaster, Mr Livingstone, took his seat at the organ and began to play the first carol, Away in a Manger – Josh's favourite which he knew off by heart. He sang with all his heart and soul and when it was finished, Mr Livingstone turned round and smiled at him. Josh felt so happy and didn't care a hoot that Paul would tease him later on.

At the end of the rehearsal, the parents began to arrive to collect the children. Josh spotted his mother who was talking to Mrs Browning. Then the choir was dismissed and Josh ran over to his mother.

Then, the dreadful thing happened!

'Joshua, you sang beautifully today,' said Mrs Browning. 'How do you feel about singing the first verse as a solo tomorrow at the concert? We could start off with you and then the others would join in?'

'Josh would love to do that,' said mother cheerfully. 'Wouldn't you, Josh? We'd all be so proud of you.'

'Oh no, mum, I couldn't, I really couldn't,' said Josh,

suddenly filled with horror of the thought of singing out front, all on his own.

'All the notes would be wrong and everyone would laugh at me.'

But Mrs Browning had already turned away to speak to another parent, and Josh's mother was anxious to speak to Paul who was going to play football at the village hall which had flood lights so that the children could play after dark in the winter months.

'Of course you can sing on your own, Josh. You always do at home. Now, don't be silly. You'll be fine tomorrow.'

'Oh Josh-U-R-a Star,' shouted Paul as he forked a sausage from the plate of sausages which mother had put on the table. 'Or rather,' he said, laughing at his own joke, 'U-R-not a Star. You're just a silly old duck quacking around the pond. Quack! Quack! Quack!' he went on waving his sausage at Josh, who put his hands over his ears so that he couldn't hear Paul's mocking voice.

'Shut up! Shut up!' he shouted back at Paul. 'Just because you can't sing, you can only shout, and you're not much good at football, either. You're jealous, that's what you are.'

'And you're just a worm, and I'm coming to gobble you up,' shouted Paul leaping towards Josh and pointing his fork at him.

'Boys, Boys, Stop that,' said mother coming into the kitchen. 'Paul, you'd better get on with your homework; and now, Josh, bath time. And early bed. You've got to be looking your best tomorrow.'

Josh couldn't eat any supper. In fact, he began to feel ill. His tummy started to hurt and he felt sick. Good, he thought. Now I won't be able to go to school tomorrow and someone else will have to sing 'Away in a Manger'.

'Nonsense,' said mother, who was beginning to lose patience with Josh and all his grumbling. 'You've got an attack of the Wobblies, that's all. You'll be alright on the night, as the Stars say.'

The Wobblies! What a horrible world, thought Josh as he climbed into his bed that night in his own little room which he was lucky to have as Paul liked to stay up late playing with his computer and now slept in the front room.

That night, Josh couldn't sleep a wink. He kept thinking about the concert and how he was going to let everyone down the next day. Would he be sick in front of the whole school he wondered as he tossed and turned in his little bed?

His mother had not drawn the curtains tightly together that night and the light from the full moon shone into Josh's bedroom. He loved the moon's big, friendly face, and, although he would never admit it to anyone, he was just a bit frightened when his room was completely in the dark.

He tried to sing 'Away in a Manger' softly to himself, but couldn't remember the words. Then he began to cry and pulled the duvet over his head so that Paul couldn't hear him.

'Now, what's all this about?' said a voice coming from somewhere in the room. 'Why are you sad, Josh? You've got nothing to cry about. You've got a warm bed, a kind mother, a big brother who loves you, although he's a bit jealous of you at the moment. You've had no supper but you can look forward to a tasty breakfast. So what's up?'

Josh stopped crying and sat up in his bed, pushing the duvet away. He stared round the room, now flooded with moonlight, and there, sitting at the end of his bed, was a lovely little boy, with golden hair brushed up into spikes on top of his head. He was wearing blue glasses which sparkled in the moonlight and there was a ring of light round his head.

Josh should have been afraid of the strange boy, but he looked so friendly that he wasn't afraid at all. In fact, he stopped crying and felt only a great peace.

'Who are you?' Josh managed to say.

'I'm Stephen, Stevie to you, and I heard you crying and decided to pop in and see what's wrong.'

'Are you an angel?' said Josh who had learnt about angels recently at school.

'Yes, you could call me an angel. I'm really a Guardian Angel and I help children who are unhappy. You seem a bit a bit down in the dumps so tell me what's wrong and I'll help you if I can.'

So Josh told Stevie all about the concert tomorrow and how Paul laughed at him and how sick he was feeling and he was afraid he would let all his friends in the choir down.

'Really?' said Stevie giving just a very tiny yawn. 'Is that all? No major tragedy then? Just a bit wobbly about singing a solo? That's not a problem. Now, do you feel sick at this moment?'

Josh thought about it. 'No, I feel fine now.'

'Good. And you'll feel fine tomorrow. I heard you singing this afternoon, you know and you've got the best

voice in the school. Go to sleep now and when you wake up tomorrow, just say to yourself, 'Today, I am going to sing like an angel.' And you will. Trust me, I'm an angel,' said Stevie giving a little cough.

'Will you be there with me tomorrow?' said Josh feeling just a bit wobbly again.

'Course I'll be there. You won't see me, of course, because I'd only get in the way. But I'll be there and you'll hear me talking to you, if you listen carefully. Now go to sleep and I'll be seeing you around. Nighty night!'

Josh wasn't frightened any more. He snuggled down under is duvet and was soon fast asleep.

That afternoon, Josh, with his hair brushed carefully and his shoes polished and wearing his dark red school pullover which his mother had washed and ironed specially for the occasion, stepped forward when it was time for the choir to sing, and he sang 'Away in a Manger' perfectly in tune and his clear, sweet voice soared away up into the high, arched roof of the church.

After the concert was over, Mr Livingstone smiled at Josh.

'Well done, Josh' he said, 'we'll have you singing in the cathedral one of these days.'

'Thanks Stevie,' thought Josh and waited for the reply.

22

'Not at all,' a small voice said. 'All part of the service. Just call me any time. 'Bye for now.'

"You Are Beautiful"

'I've had a message from a little girl in Oakfield,' said Stevie, dipping a spoon into a pot of Angels' honey and preparing to pop it into his mouth.

Stevie and Angelina were perched up on their cloud talking about any problems they were having in their part of Sussex.

'Something for you to tackle, I think,' said Stevie. 'You might have to do a bit of shape-shifting.'

'Since when have you been given permission to give me orders?' said Angelina, gently taking the spoonful of honey away from Stevie and popping the contents into her own mouth.

'Here, give over! That's my honey!' said Stevie. 'Go and get your own pot. The shop's always open.'

'Too late, I've eaten it,' said Angelina gleefully. You should wake up, Stevie. What's wrong with you today?'

'I need a break, that's all. Too many unhappy children to sort out and too many bossy girl angels stealing my honey! I suggest you tune in to this little girl and do some work for a change. Her name is Lucy and she thinks she's ugly. Just up your street, I think.'

(Angels, you know, don't possess mobile phones and can't send e-mails. Instead, they have special brains that can tune into our thoughts. You could say that angels have brain waves! All they have to do is switch on their brains to 'Receive messages' and then switch to another channel in their brains to 'Send messages.' Clever, aren't they?

Also, they can change their shape, too. Sometimes, they can appear as another person – a grandmother, say, or a teacher, or a friendly animal. Guardian angels are always friendly. Bad angels, who serve Malus Maximus can change their shapes, too, but they only pretend to be good and are easily recognised.)

Stevie and Angelina shared their pot of Angels' honey and Angelina switched her brain over to 'Receive', whilst Stevie settled down on his cloud, folded down his little wings and went fast asleep. Everyone needs sleep; even angels!

'Lucy, time to get up,' said her Lucy's mother, pulling back the duvet on her bed. 'You're going to be late for school again and I've got a lot of needy people waiting for me to help them get dressed.'

'I don't want to go to school,' said Lucy, who was in the top class of her primary school. Oakfield was in the next village to Maryfield and had its own primary school which was a big school and pupils came from other surrounding villages.

'I don't feel well. And I'm still tired.'

'Oh Lucy, please be sensible. There's nothing wrong with you and you know I can't leave you here all on your own. What's the matter? Why don't you want to go to school?'

'Because I'm ugly and everyone hates me. They say I'm too fat. Pete called me a fat sausage and he said he wants to cover me with tomato sauce and eat me!'

Lucy's mother could hardly believe what she was hearing.

'Lucy, my beautiful little girl, don't take any notice of those horrid big boys. You're just perfect. Now get dressed quickly and I'll make you some lovely toast and honey, instead of your usual cereal, and you'll feel better straight away.'

'I don't want any breakfast. I want to be thin. Only thin girls are beautiful, Pete says.'

'Then I shall have to have a word with this Pete,' said mother firmly. 'And I shall write a letter to Mrs. Manning. Just ignore Pete and join up with your friends.'

'I haven't got any friends,' said Lucy as she climbed out of bed and made for the bathroom.

Lucy was the only child of Jenny and her partner, Dave. She was clever and funny and everyone liked her. She had curly red hair and a round, smiling face, with a sprinkling of freckles across her nose. Usually, she loved going to school, and joined in all the games as well as working hard at her lessons. That is, until Pete started to call her nasty names and all his friends began laughing at her.

Lucy tried to take no notice of them, but, one day, she looked at herself in the mirror in the changing room at the swimming pool and decided that there was too much fat on her tummy. Her legs, she thought, looked like tree trunks. That was it! She was too fat, she thought. Pete was right. She was ugly.

She looked at some magazines which her mother had brought home and saw how beautiful the girls were. They were all thin, really thin, and they all wore beautiful clothes and everyone looked at them and cheered when they showed off their clothes.

'Well,' thought Lucy, 'I am going to be thin, like these girls. No more toast for me, or cereal. No more biscuits or chocolate, or ice-cream or pizzas.'

And Lucy began to lose weight!

Soon she could wrap her school skirt round her instead of doing up the buttons at the side. She began to feel tired all the time and fell asleep in Mrs Manning's history lesson. Lucy's mother started to worry about her and went to see Mrs Manning, who said Lucy was "going through a phase" and would soon start eating again when she got really hungry.

But Lucy didn't start eating again. Not proper eating.

She ate only a lettuce leaf and a tomato for supper and only drank water.

She soon lost even more weight and began to feel very ill indeed. Then, one day, when her mother said she must go and see a doctor, Lucy sent up a prayer to her guardian angel.

'Please come and help me,' she said. 'I don't know what to do.'

That was the prayer Angelina picked up.

Lucy's mother wasn't the only person worried about her. Her grandmother came to see her one day and was so shocked to see her lovely granddaughter looking so thin and pale that she said she would come and stay for a few days and help Jenny and Dave for a bit.

Lucy loved her granny and was so pleased to see her. At first, granny didn't say anything about how thin Lucy had become. She pretended everything was normal and told Jenny that Lucy was growing up to be a 'real beauty'.

Then, one day, after Lucy had had a really horrid day at school, granny came and sat on the edge of Lucy's bed and Lucy cuddled up to her.

'Now then, what's up? What's going wrong with you? Let me help you. You know I'm always on your side. I'm your guardian angel, you know and I'll never let you down. Now, start at the beginning.'

So Lucy poured out all her troubles, how she was teased at school by Pete and his friends, and now she hated going to school and...here Lucy paused for a moment... she had nothing to wear to Emmie's party on Saturday.

'Is Emmie your friend?' said granny.

'Yes.'

'A good friend?'

'Yes. And she's beautiful and everyone likes her and she's not fat and ugly like me.'

'I see,' said granny smiling a little smile. 'Well, you must go to her party and I'll make you beautiful. You'll see. Now, I've made you some banana sandwiches and mummy will be home soon, so let's give her a surprise, shall we? Here, let me brush your hair. Look, I've found this hair clip of mine which I thought you might like. I used to wear it when I was a little girl. Come on, let's go for it, shall we?'

The hair clip was in the shape of a beautiful blue butterfly, the colour of a summer sky. Granny brushed out Lucy's red curls and pinned them back with the butterfly brooch. Lucy put on her old leggings and a

baggy tee-shirt and went downstairs with granny to eat the banana sandwiches. Suddenly, she felt hungry. Granny had made some tomato soup which was Lucy's favourite and Lucy helped granny make a big salad for when her mother came home.

Emmie's party was on the Saturday of the half-term break. On Friday, granny woke Lucy up early and told her to get dressed quickly as they were going to look at some shops to buy Lucy a party outfit.

'Now that you're sensible and eating food again, you'll be the Belle of the Ball. That's what we used to say when someone came to a party looking smart. You'll be a right Bobby Dazzler as my mother used to say to me. I loved going to parties and you'll enjoy Emmie's party, you'll see.'

'Can I be a Bobby Dazzler, granny?' said Lucy springing out of bed.

'Course you can. Breakfast first, though.'

On Saturday, Lucy put on the bright green skirt which granny had bought her and the little daffodil yellow tee shirt. Mummy had bought her some wonderful yellow shoes with a sparkling pattern on them. With her red hair neatly pinned back with granny's hair clip, Lucy set off for Emmie's house. And, do you know, she had a wonderful time and ate two slices of birthday cake and danced with all her friends; even with Pete, who had stopped teasing her.

On the way home, in granny's car, Lucy said to her grandmother, 'Am I a Bobby Dazzler, too, granny? Just like you were?'

'Of course you are,' said granny. 'Just like me.'

'Well done, Angelina,' said Stevie, back On Call again. 'You did a great job with Lucy. Any more messages from her?'

'Just happy ones,' said Angelina. 'Now, it's my turn to have a nap. All this shape-shifting is a bit exhausting. Your turn next, Stevie. Let's hope you do as good a job as I did; if I might say so.'

Harry And A Wolf Called Sid

It was getting late and would soon be dark. Harry was bored and wanted to go home, but his mother was busy talking to her friend, Janet, about the arrangements for a Hallowe'en party they were planning. His big brother, Dick, and his friend, Jason, had stopped playing football and were now building a tree house. Harry had wanted to help them but Dick had called down to him, 'Clear off, Harry. House building is not for six year olds. You'd only fall out of the back door and hurt yourself. Don't be a nuisance. Go away.'

So Harry had wandered back to where his mother was sitting with her friend, and picked up his big story book

with all the pictures in it. He opened it at the story he liked best about a boy and a girl who, whilst they were walking in a wood, came across a wonderful house. The house was made of sweets and biscuits and was called The Gingerbread House. There was a lovely

35

picture of the house with its walls shining with boiled sweets and the tiles on the roof were made of jam tarts. Looking at this house made Harry feel hungry. They'd eaten all the picnic food and the empty basket was packed away in Janet's car along with her family dog who was now curled up in the boot of the car asleep. They were all ready to go home, if only the mothers would stop talking and the boys would come down from their tree.

Harry looked up from his book and glanced at the trees surrounding the grassy patch which the two families were using as a camp. Then he had an idea! His mother had started talking to someone on her mobile phone and Janet was listening to what she was talking about. The boys had disappeared into their tree house. Harry closed the book and laid it down on the grass. Yes, he thought, it was a good idea. So he stood up, and walked towards the trees. No one stopped him. No one seemed to care where he went, he thought sadly. They were all too busy with their own affairs. He was going to find another gingerbread house and he would bring them back pieces of the gingerbread wall and some of the jam tarts from the roof. He would have his own adventure, he thought. Then they would all notice him and make a fuss of him and thank him for giving them all the lovely sweet treats.

Harry was a sturdy little boy, big for his age, and always curious to find out how things worked and why people did what they did and said what they said. And why his mother was always talking to people on her mobile phone instead of talking to him! That day, he was wearing his jeans and his old trainers as his mother didn't want him to spoil his new trainers with the winking lights on their heels. As it was getting colder now, his mother had insisted he wore his fleecy jacket and had zipped him up firmly inside it. However, he couldn't be bothered to look for his red woolly hat. He wasn't going far, he thought, and would be back long before it got any darker.

Once he had left sight of his family party, he began to feel excited and very grown up. He was off on his own! On a real adventure! There was a path through the trees and he felt sure this would lead him to the gingerbread house. The trees on either side of the path looked to him like sentries on guard duty, and he waved to them. They were shedding their leaves and, as he went further into the wood, the path disappeared under a thick layer of fallen leaves. This was great fun, he thought, as he began to kick the leaves up in the air and shouted in excitement. He didn't notice that the sun had now vanished, and it

was getting darker by the minute. He didn't notice that the path had also vanished and he was walking about without any idea where he was going. Never mind, he thought, he would soon find the house and then he would simply go back the way he'd come.

He was a brave little boy but not brave enough though, when, from a tree near him, an owl hooted. He looked up and saw its large, white face staring down at him. Suddenly, he began to be afraid. Something rustled in the leaves near him and he began to think of all the creatures that lived in the wood – not only squirrels and badgers, which he liked, but, and here he began to feel really frightened, he'd heard that wolves liked to live in woods, and wolves, he felt certain, would like to eat little boys;  especially sturdy little boys wandering around on their own! There were always wolves in the story books and they were always up to no good.

Harry then decided it was time to go back to the others. The gingerbread house could wait for another time. Now that the sun had disappeared, it had turned cold and he was hungry. He turned round and began to run back along what he thought was the path. After a while he didn't seem to be getting anywhere and he was tired and wanted to see his mother again. Even Dick and Jason would be welcome now. If only he'd brought his torch with him – his new torch which his father had given him!

He ran on through the trees, trying to fight back his tears as he was really frightened now. Suddenly, he found the ground give way beneath his feet and he found himself falling down a steep bank. He tried to stop himself by grasping an overhanging branch, but the branch came away in his hand and he fell onto a pile of dry leaves. As he tried to stand up, he felt a sharp pain in his foot and realised that he had twisted his ankle whilst he was falling and now his foot hurt very badly. He began to feel very cold and wished he'd put on his hat. He began to shiver and called out for his family.

'Mum, dad,' he called out, and then, 'Dick, please come, please. I've hurt myself and can't walk.'

But no-one came. Just silence, then a rustle of some small creatures amongst the leaves. Then he thought of those wolves. Were there wolves in England? he thought. He'd never met anyone who'd seen a wolf. Maybe they were only in story books, not real at all. A bit like dragons. No-one he knew had ever seen a dragon, yet story books were always full of dragons and other strange beasts.

Trying to be brave, he began to cover himself up with leaves. They would keep him warm, he thought, until someone came along and found him. So he curled up under his duvet of leaves and began to cry quietly to himself. To stop all those nasty thoughts about wolves and dragons, he tried to think about the other book, which his teacher had shown him only the other day. It had lots of lovely pictures in it of angels, she called them, beautiful creatures with light shining round their heads.

He didn't think they were real but, at least, he could try calling out to them and maybe one of them would hear him and come to his rescue. So he said out loud, 'Please angels, if you are really out there, please send someone to rescue me. Please!'

And then he heard the sound of leaves rustling nearby. There was no wind, so it had to be some sort of creature creeping towards him. He heard the creature breathing too – a panting sort of breathing as if the creature had been in a hurry to get to him.

'Oh no,' he whispered. 'Please, angel, don't make it a wolf! Not a wolf!'

He tried to crouch down further under the leaves so that the creature out there, wouldn't see him. Harry didn't know very much about animals, because animals don't have to see, they rely on their noses. They can smell things we can't and never will be able to smell. And this animal, whatever it was, could certainly smell Harry!

He heard the sound of more panting and dry leaves crackling and he opened one eye, and then the other. And there it was! A dark shape, crouching above him at the top of the bank. He could see the outline of the creature. It had big ears and and a long tail and two eyes that shone in the darkness like bicycle lamps.

It was a wolf, thought Harry. A horrible, hungry wolf! The angel hadn't heard him. Help! Help! He called out.

Then he heard a strange noise – a soft, whiney sort of noise, like the noise a squeaky gate makes when it needs oiling. Next, the creature gave a little bark and began to slide down the bank towards Harry. When he reached Harry, the creature pawed back the leaves from his face and gave him a big lick. Harry stopped crying and stared at the animal in astonishment. It wasn't a wolf. It was a Labrador dog, and he belonged to his mother's friend. Then Harry remembered his name. It was Sid.

'Sid, Sid,' he said, sitting up and brushing off the leaves. 'Clever Sid! Look, I've hurt my foot and I can't walk. Please go back and get mummy. Good dog. Good dog.'

Sid gave Harry's face another lick and leapt up the bank, barking as he went.

Harry didn't have to wait long. Soon, a familiar figure was standing at the top of the bank. It was dad! Mummy must have called him up on her mobile, he thought, and he'd come to find him.

Harry pushed back the leaves and began to crawl up the bank, calling out to his father. He came sliding down the bank and picked up Harry and gave him a big hug.

'Well, what have you been up to? I see you've hurt your foot. Now, let's get you back to the others and you can tell us all what happened. I think you've had enough adventures for one day, don't you? But why did you go off on your own?'

'I wanted to find the gingerbread house,' said Harry clinging on tightly to his father's shoulder.

'Another time we'll all go looking for it. And now, say thank you to Sid, here. He's the one who found you.'

'The angel sent him to me,' said Harry looking down at Sid who was trotting along beside him. 'I thought he was a wolf to begin with.'

'An angel, you say? Must have been your guardian angel sent him. The trouble with you, Harry is that you look at too many picture books. Now, let's see if there's a biscuit in my pocket for Sid. I think he deserves a reward, don't you?'

'He certainly does,' said Harry. 'He's the cleverest dog in all the world.'

Always Trust A Dolphin

It was another perfect day of a perfect holiday. The sun was shining down from a sky, the colour of forget-me-nots, onto a brilliant turquoise-coloured sea where the little white yacht, called the Saint Christopher, was bobbing gently up and down as it made its way to the little island where they were to stop and have a picnic lunch. Isabella, aged eleven, had never before felt as happy as she was that day. Mummy and daddy were staying back in the hotel on Skopelos, the Greek island where they were enjoying a wonderful holiday before Isabella started at her big school in September. And now, here she was, with her new friends, Irene and David and their mother and father, who owned the yacht and were teaching her how to sail.

Isabella had met Irene and David by the hotel swimming pool and had immediately become friends. They had invited Isabella and her parents to sail on their boat that day, but Isabella's mother had wanted to be lazy and have a quiet day by the hotel's pool, and Isabella's father said he felt lazy, too, and would stay with her. So Isabella went off on her own with her new friends.

It was very warm, despite the slight breeze that had

taken them away from the big island towards the smaller island which they could see in the distance. Isabella and Irene were wearing their bikinis – Isabella's was bright pink with white spots on it, which suited her sun-tanned skin and long brown hair which she had tied back into a pony tail. Irene was very fair skinned and had to put on some sun cream to stop herself from burning and wore a sun hat to cover her short blond hair and was putting on a shirt over her white bikini. Irene's mother had put on a bathing costume as they were all planning to swim ashore.

It was so peaceful, just the sound of gentle waves tapping at the side of the boat. David had let Isabella sail the boat on her own towards the island and she felt very

proud. She loved watching the white sails fill out and send the little yacht skimming over the water. As they drew nearer the island, she could just see the patch of white sand making a beach between the grey rocks.

'That's where we're going,' said David, pointing to the beach. 'There's a small cafe there where we can buy drinks and mum's made us lots of sandwiches. What do you think of that, Bella?' he said. (Her friends had called her Bella and she didn't mind at all. It made her feel very grown up.)

'I'll take over now, because we're going to drop anchor and then we'll all go ashore.'

David took the helm from Isabella, who sat down next to Irene. She was so happy to be there with her new friends. She wished they could sail on for ever.

And then the thought entered her head.

'How are we going to get to the island?' she said to Irene, who looked at her in astonishment.

'Why, we'll swim there, of course. You're a brilliant swimmer. I've seen you swimming in the hotel and you beat us all. You swim just like one of those dolphins we're always catching sight of.'

'But I've never swum in the sea,' said Isabella, suddenly feeling a bit wobbly. 'There might be jelly fish

about, or a giant squid,' she
whispered, ashamed of her fear,
but unable to stop it.

Irene's dad heard her and bust
out laughing.

'No giant squids here. Only
ten minutes and we'll be on the island. We're going to
drop anchor now.'

Isabella helped to make the yacht secure and she did
her best to laugh and join in with the others as they
lowered the sails, but she felt terrified as she thought of
jumping into the sea where she would be out of her
depth, and maybe, just maybe, there would be a giant
squid waiting for her.

When the boat was secure, Irene and her family
jumped into the sea with shouts of delight and set off
towards the island. Irene's mother was more cautious.
She had put the sandwiches in a water-proof bag and
hung it round her neck and she lowered herself into the
water. Now she turned and looked back at Isabella who
was standing at the side of the boat gazing down into the
water.

'Sure you're all right, Bella?' she called out. 'Come
and join us when you're ready. It's quite safe. David will

keep an eye on you and come to your rescue if you need him.'

Then they were all gone, just three little heads bobbing around on the water and Irene's mother doing a sort of three legged doggy paddle as she tried to keep the bag of sandwiches out of the sea.

Irene took a last look and decided to go down into the cabin and pretend to feel ill. 'I can't jump,' she whispered to herself, 'I really can't.'

Just then, something caught her eye. It was a grey triangular shape that had suddenly appeared out of the sea, and it was coming towards the yacht. 'A shark!' she thought. 'Help, help, a shark!'

A shark, she knew, could attack a boat and she had nothing to defend herself with, except a boat hook, which the shark could easily snap in two. Then she thought of the name of the yacht – Saint Christopher.

'Please, please, Saint Christopher,' she whispered, 'Come and help me.'

The fin suddenly came to a halt just near the boat and then, with a great splash, the rest of the body reared up out of the sea. It wasn't a shark. It was a big, shining dolphin with tiny twinkling eyes and a broad smile on its face.

Isabella stared at it in wonder. The dolphin was so beautiful, so friendly, that she didn't feel at all afraid. She leaned over the side of the boat and patted the creature's shining, grey head.

'What's the matter with you?' she thought she heard the dolphin say.

'I don't want to go ashore,' she said.

'Don't want to, or afraid to?' said the dolphin, opening its wide mouth in a friendly smile.

'I don't like swimming,' said Isabella.

'Rubbish! Everyone likes swimming. Especially attractive young ladies, like you.'

Isabella had never been called attractive before, or a young lady, for that matter. She began to like this dolphin.

'I like swimming in pools,' she said, 'where you know when you are out of your depth and can see the bottom of the pool and know there are no nasty creatures waiting to bite me.'

'Well, there are no nasty creatures here, either. Just a few jelly fish, but you can always keep away from those. There's me, of course, and my family out there, he said, nodding his head towards some dolphins leaping about in the water.

'I'm friendly, all dolphins like humans, you know. I'll tell you what we'll do. You will jump into the sea – you can do that, can't you? I'm sure you've jumped off the side of the pool many times, haven't you?'

Isabella nodded agreement. 'When you're in the sea,' the dolphin went on, 'you grab hold of my tail and I'll take you into the shallow water and you can join your friends. Friends ought to keep together, like my family out there. Now, stop thinking about it. Just jump. One, two, three, JUMP!'

And Isabella jumped.

At first she felt terrified as the water closed over her head, but, when she bobbed up to the surface and saw in front of her the dolphin's beautiful fan-shaped tail, she

knew she was safe. She grasped the tail firmly in her hands, and the dolphin set off. As they skimmed over the water Isabella felt she was sail boarding and shouted with delight. The dolphin playfully flicked its tail and then leapt up into the air with Isabella holding on tightly. She wanted to climb onto his back and ride him like a pony, but he seemed to know what she was thinking because he flicked his tail in disapproval making her hold on even more tightly.

When they were into the shallow water off the island, she felt the dolphin leap into the air again and then he flicked his tail very strongly; so strongly that she let go and fell back into the water. The dolphin then bounded off, leaping up and down, circling around her as she trod water wanting him to come back. But he didn't come back. Instead, he turned with a graceful leap and grinned at her.

'You're on your own now, little girl. You can swim that little distance, can't you? Look, your friends are waving to you.'

Sure enough, Irene and David were waving to her from the beach and Isabella suddenly found herself swimming towards them. No trouble at all! All the terror gone. Just a wonderful happy feeling. She's done it! Of course she had. She was a good swimmer. Everyone said that.

'Well done, Isabella,' said David who had rushed to help her ashore. 'We told you it was safe to swim in the sea. No giant squids. No jelly fish.'

'Just a beautiful dolphin,' said David's mother coming over to help.

'Come and get a drink. You must be thirsty after that dolphin ride.'

'He was my guardian angel,' said Isabella, squeezing the water out of her hair.

'Since when did a guardian angel look like a dolphin?' said David.

Isabell laughed. 'I reckon they can look like anything they choose. Just depends where and when they are needed.'

The sun continued to shine that day and when the time came to go back to the hotel, Isabella swam with the others back to the yacht and got there first.

'I love swimming,' she told her parents, when she joined them at the hotel.

'Especially in the sea.'

'Really?' said her mother. 'What about sharks?'

'Sharks? Who's afraid of sharks when there is a dolphin on call?'

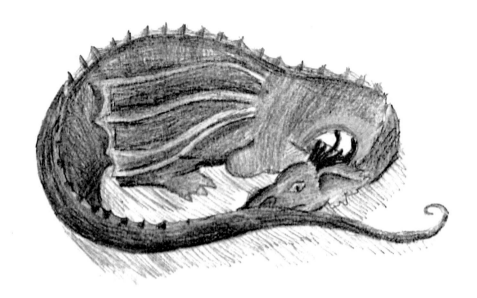

Smiling Faces

In a deep, dark cave in the middle of a rocky desert lived a big, ugly dragon. His name was Malus Maximus. We'll call him Old Maxie.

He was the enemy of The Holy One and Michael and all the good angels, like Stevie and Angelina.

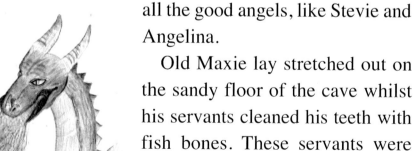

Old Maxie lay stretched out on the sandy floor of the cave whilst his servants cleaned his teeth with fish bones. These servants were little creatures, called demons, who

had plump bodies, like piglets, with long, flicky tails and pig faces with two little horns between their ears. Two of these demons, called Pincher and Poker were brushing and polishing Old Maxie's scaly body which lay coiled around him on the floor like a giant python. Old Maxie was a bit of a dandy and liked looking his best at all times.

Suddenly, he yawned, opening his mouth, as big as a crocodile, and flicking the teeth-cleaning demons onto the floor. Then he took a deep breath and puffed out some little clouds of smoke.

'That's better,' he growled. 'That goat you gave me for dinner was a bit tough. Now where is everybody? I want to hold a Council of War. Call Grin and Groaner, Snakebite and Snuffle, Sneezer and Snearer. On second thoughts, I'll wake them up. Stand back, you lot.'

Pincher and Poker scuttled off to the back of the cave whilst Old Maxie uncoiled his scaly body, threw back his crocodile head and let out an angry roar that echoed round the cave and woke up all the lazy demons.

They came rushing up to where Old Maxie was lying and sat themselves down cross-legged on the floor, like children in a school assembly.

'Are you ready?' bellowed Old Maxie. 'Then sing our song. Ready? After three.'

The demons obediently chanted One, Two, Three and then sang the Song of the Demons.

'Long live Maxie!'

'Long live Our Master.'

'May he live for ever!'

'May he crush his enemies.'

'Maxie the Great! Maxie the Mighty!'

The last sentence was sung as loudly as they could, but Old Maxie wasn't satisfied and bellowed at them to sing it again.

'Louder!' he yelled. 'Louder!'

So off they went again, shouting out the words and beating the floor with their tails, until the walls of the cave shook and bits of stone came tumbling down from the roof.

'That's enough,' roared Old Maxie. 'Now, listen to me. I've heard from my spies that too many stupid children have been saved by our enemy who calls himself The Holy One. Holy One indeed! That's a laugh. He thinks he's very clever, but we can be cleverer than him and all his ridiculous angels, can't we Friends?'

Lots of the demons had stopped listening to Old Maxie and were looking anxiously at the walls of the cave to see if more stones were going to come tumbling down on them. Old Maxie saw them looking away from him and flicked his tail with annoyance and began to puff more smoke out of his nostrils like a volcano about to erupt.

'Can't we Friends?' he bellowed, making them all jump with fright.

'Yes, Master' they shouted back.

'Again!'

'Yes Master!' they roared and Old Maxie puffed out some more smoke, making Snuffle and Sneezer start a fit of coughing.

'That's enough of that, you two. As you've drawn attention to yourselves, you can be the ones to do some shape-shifting. Get down to a village called Oakfield in Sussex and look out for a child called Victoria. My spies tell me that she's proud and thinks she's special just because she's got a pretty face. She needs taking down a peg or two. See what you can do.'

Snuffle and Sneezer looked at each other in dismay. Why, Oh Why, did they have to start coughing at that moment? But there was no getting away from it. When Old Maxie gave orders, he had to be obeyed.

'I hear Old Maxie's up to his tricks again,' said Stevie to his friend, Angelina. They were sitting on their little cloud, apart from the others, eating Angelic sausages dipped in honey.

'How do you know that, Stevie?' said Angelina, stopping a sausage on its way into her mouth.

'One of the spies, Dickon, has just contacted me. He's picked up a brain wave from one of Old Maxie's demons who apparently forgot to switch off the brain wave after he's sent it. I don't like this. They mentioned Oakfield, by the way and that's on our patch.'

'You or me?' said Angelina, popping the sausage into her mouth.

'Both of us,' I think. 'This sounds serious...'

Victoria was in the school's changing room tying up her shoe laces when her friend Lisa's mobile phone rang.

'Who is it?' she said.

'It's my mum. She's got to go and see Gran who's fallen over in the garden and hurt her leg. I'm to go home by myself, for once. Sheila from next door will come and keep me company until mum comes home. Will you be all right going home on your own, Vicky?'

'Of course. I've not far to go. In fact, just the next road after the school.'

Usually, Victoria and Lisa left school together and Lisa's mother picked them up at the school gates and drove them both home. But today, things were different.

The two girls were the last to leave Oakfield School as they had been to an after-school dancing class. They hadn't bothered to change out of their dancing clothes, leggings and a loose T shirt, their hair tied back with sparkly clips. Both were in the top class of their school and both were cheerful, friendly girls with not a care in the world.

At the school gate, Lisa waved goodbye to Victoria and ran off towards her home in Watkins Drive.

Victoria turned the other way and set off for her home in Eastwood Close. She walked quickly along, clutching her bag with her home clothes in it, humming the tune of the last dance. Then she noticed the big, white car again. She'd seen it before when she left school with Lisa's mother and she had always thought it was someone's rich father coming to pick up his child from school. She'd never seen it stop, however. The driver just drove slowly past the school as if looking for someone. Today, there was no-one about.

The man in the car waved to Victoria as he drove past her and stopped a little way ahead. She saw him open his window and thought he was going to ask her if she had seen his son or daughter.

Victoria was a bright, outgoing girl. She liked helping people, so when the man opened his car door, she went up to him and asked him if he needed any help.

'Thank you. It's very kind of you to offer to help me. I'm looking for the Oakfield Stores. I've been told you can buy bread and milk there and something for supper.'

'Oh yes, it's in my road, Eastwood Close. It's not far from here. Only five minutes in this big car of yours.'

'You like my car?' said the man. He was not a young man, quite old, in fact, thought Victoria. Not unlike her grandfather. He had a pink, smiley face and just a fringe of grey hair on his head. He was wearing a grey suit and a pale blue shirt and a very pretty blue silk tie.

'It's a beautiful car,' said Victoria, who liked cars. 'What make is it?'

'It's a Mercedes. It's very comfortable. Look at my leather seats.'

'It's lovely. But I must go now or else mummy will be worried about me.'

The man then got out of the car and opened the door to the back seat.

'Why don't you get in and I'll take you home. Then you can show me where the shop is.'

Victoria hesitated. She heard her mother's voice speaking to her inside her head.

'Never accept a lift from someone you don't know.'

However, this man was so nice and so old. Surely he wouldn't harm anyone. He had such a lovely smiling face and he'd been eating a chocolate bar, she noticed. The empty wrapper was in the glove compartment. And there was another bar of chocolate alongside it.

'It's not far. I'd rather walk,' said sensible Victoria.

'Oh, jump in. You can have my second bar of chocolate, if you like. It will be a reward for being kind to me.'

Still she hesitated. Then the man with the smiling face

took a step towards her and laid a hand on her arm. She tried to draw back but her held on to her tightly.

'Don't be afraid, little girl. You'll enjoy the ride.'

Suddenly a voice behind them made Victoria jump out of her skin.

'Stop that at once! Victoria, who is this man? Do you know him?'

Victoria turned and saw old Mrs Bealey standing there with her scruffy dog called Reggie. Reggie was tugging at the end of his lead to get to her. Victoria knew Mrs Bealey. She lived next door to Victoria's house and her family called the Old Beetle because she had black hair and wore black-rimmed glasses, and always wore a shiny black raincoat in all weathers.

Mrs Bealey hung onto Reggie's lead with one hand and with the other, she took out her mobile phone from her coat pocket.

'He's only going to take me home, Mrs Bealey,' said Victoria. 'He's only being kind.'

'Hmm! Better come along with me. At least you've seen me before.'

'Let Victoria make up her own mind,' said the smiley man, pushing Victoria towards the car door.

'I think you'd better get in that car of yours and drive

away. Let Victoria go, or else I shall call the police.'

'You mind your own business, you old crow,' said the man, no longer smiling. The police have better things to do than listen to you. In you get, Victoria,' he said, giving her a push.

Well, Reggie had recognized Victoria and saw she was

in trouble. He'd seen the man push Victoria into the car and he didn't approve of this. So, with a very nasty growl, Reggie leapt towards the man. Mrs Bealey released the lead and Reggie jumped up at the man and fastened his teeth into the sleeve of the man's jacket.

'Get him off me,' yelled the man.

'Only if I say so,' said Mrs Bealey. 'He will bite you, too, if I tell him to. Good dog, Reggie.'

Reggie growled and showed his teeth to show he was ready and willing.

The man let go of Victoria, slammed the door to the back seat, and jumped into the driver's seat. Then he drove off, very fast indeed.

'Thank you, Mrs Bealey,' said Victoria who now was feeling a bit frightened. 'And thank you, Reggie,' she said, stooping to pat the dog who was now whining with pleasure and licking her hand, now that she was safe.

'I'm glad I came along,' said Mrs Bealey. 'Never accept lifts from people you don't know. Have you ever seen that man before, Victoria?'

'Once or twice. He drives up and down this road looking for someone. He's very nice and was going to give me a chocolate bar.'

'Was he, now? Well, come along. I'll take you home.

Reggie would like a biscuit, wouldn't you, Reggie?'

Reggie gave a bark of approval and they set off home. Victoria, who was really a bright little girl asked Mrs Bealey if she had noticed the number plate on the man's car.

'Of course,' said Mrs Bealey. 'And, once you're safely indoors I am going to phone the police and give them the number. That's what detectives do in Crime films on television, isn't it?'

Victoria, who never watched Crime films nodded in agreement. There was more to Mrs Bealey than she had ever imagined.

'Phew, that was a close shave,' said Stevie, back with Angelina on their cloud. 'Old Maxie really is on the war path. We did well there, didn't we?'

'You were great as Reggie, Stevie,' said Angelina giving him a hug.

'You weren't so bad yourself as old Barbara Bealey. I expect Victoria's family might ask her in for a cup of tea occasionally from now on.'

'And there will always be a biscuit for Reggie.' Said Angelina.

That's What Pockets Are For

The village of Maryfield was lucky to have a village shop which happened to be close to the school. At half past three the parents would arrive to pick up their children from school and often they would stop at the shop to buy milk and bread, or something for tea, and, maybe, if they were in luck the children could choose a bar of chocolate or packet of sweets to eat on their way home.

Charley was one of these lucky children. That day, mummy had come to collect him from school and they were going to walk home as the car was being serviced and dad was going to collect it later on.

Charley was a bright, cheerful boy and popular with the other children. He was eight years old, sturdily built, good at all sports, and he liked chocolate. Also, he was always hungry. That afternoon, he was wearing his school uniform as usual, grey trousers and a red pullover and, because the weather had turned cold, he was wearing his anorak with its big pockets full of all the useful things boys like to collect: a long piece of strong string, a piece of sticky plaster, a notebook and a biro. Charley wanted to be a detective when he grew up so he was always observing things, particularly car number plates and writing the numbers down in his notebook. One day, he might see something suspicious and help the police solve a crime.

Mummy and Charley began their walk home. They came to the shop and mummy decided she needed some more milk and cheese which she was making for their tea. She stopped and Charley was delighted with the diversion. They climbed the steps up to the door of the shop and mummy pushed it open. They were the only people in the shop that day as most of the children went home in the family car, especially in the cold weather. It was warm in the shop and mummy was soon chatting away with Sylvia who was the owner of the shop.

Mummy and Sylvia knew each other very well as they both went to the same Keep Fit class at the Village Hall and Sylvia wanted to show mummy some new scarves she had on display at the back of the shop.

'Mum,' began Charley looking at his mother appealingly.

Mummy looked at Charley. 'All right. Choose a bar of chocolate. Just one, mind, as we've got a bit of a walk ahead of us.'

So Charley began to examine the rows of different chocolate bars and packets of sweets set out temptingly

on the counter in front of him. They all looked wonderful to a little boy who was hungry. He could smell the smooth, comforting smell of the chocolate bars and imagine the flavour of the boiled sweets. Just one bar, his mother had said. What a problem! Too much choice!

Then he had an idea. He glanced round the shop. No-one had come in, mummy and Sylvia had gone to the back of the shop. What was to stop him helping himself to a second bar of chocolate and putting it in his anorak pocket? Sylvia wouldn't notice that a few bars of chocolate had disappeared. There were hundreds of sweets on display. He selected the bar of chocolate which his mother had said he could have, a Yorkie bar, and put it on top of the counter where his mother would soon put the other things she wanted to buy.

Mummy and Sylvia were still looking at the scarves. Quickly, he picked up another Yorkie bar and slipped it into his anorak pocket. Then, in went a Crunchie bar and then a Kit Kat. This was great fun, he thought. He might even share some of his loot with Simon from next door who was his friend although they went to different schools. Soon his anorak was feeling a bit heavy, so he patted his bulging pocket and decided there was room for just one more bar of chocolate. He picked up a Mars bar. Simon, he knew, liked Mars bars.

'I think you should put all those sweets back where they came from,' said a quiet voice behind him.

Charley turned round quickly, feeling his face turn bright red with embarrassment.

'You haven't paid for them, have you? We have a

69

name for people like you. You are a thief; that's what you are. If you were older, I would call a policeman and you would go to prison. But I shan't do that because I know you are really an honest young man and just this once you couldn't resist temptation. Now, take those sweets out of you pockets and put them all back where they came from.'

Charley saw a young man standing behind him. He was tall with a friendly, smiling face, a shock of yellow hair standing up straight like the prickles on a hedgehog, and bright blue eyes covered by a pair of sparkly glasses. He was wearing jeans and a white T shirt with a pattern of the stars and the moon decorating the front. Charley felt no fear of him at all, but somehow he knew there would be no use arguing with him. However, he felt he had to defend himself somehow.

'There are a lot of sweets here,' he said to the young man. 'Sylvia won't miss them. Besides, that's what pockets are for, aren't they? To put things in, I mean.'

'Really? I thought pockets were for putting your own possessions in – things you've bought with your own pocket money, or presents people have bought for you. Those chocolate bars are not yours until you've paid for them. If Sylvia allowed everyone to help themselves to her sweets, then she'd have to close the shop as she'd have no money to buy other things. Now, put those sweets back on the display and I won't tell anyone. Quick, now, before your mother comes back. If she knows what you've done, you'll be in real trouble.'

There was no more arguing. Charley's mother had made her choice out of the pile of scarves and would soon be back with him. Charley, his face still red got the bars of chocolates out of his pockets and quickly replaced them on the display.

'Good boy,' said the young man. 'Don't do it again. Now, I can't watch you all the time, but if, in future, you feel yourself being tempted to do something wrong then just call on me and I'll make you change your mind.'

'I don't know who you are,' said Charley.

'Just call me Stevie. I'll pick up the thought wave and come to your rescue.'

'What do you do? And where do you live?' said Charley. There was no-one in the shop when we came in, except Sylvia, of course. When did you come in?'

'I'm your guardian angel and I live with all the other angels and we come from everywhere. I'm sent where I am ordered, and I was needed today here in Mayfield. Goodbye Charley and, remember, don't give in to temptation; it only leads to trouble.'

'Goodbye, Stevie, and thank you,' whispered Charley watching his mother and Sylvia coming back to the main counter.

'Talking to yourself, Charley?' said his mother smiling at him and holding up a bright blue and gold scarf which she was going to buy.

'Just counting up the bars of chocolate, that's all,' said Charley, turning to wave goodbye to Stevie. To his surprise, there was no-one there and the door of the shop was still firmly shut.

'I see you've chosen a Yorkie bar,' said his mother. 'Good boy. Why don't you put another one with it and then you can give one to Simon when you go round to play with him.'

'Thank you again, Stevie,' whispered Charley, to himself, this time. It was better to have two paid-for bars of chocolate than six stolen ones, any time. He could now laugh with his mother and look Sylvia in the face without that horrible sick feeling which comes when you are feeling guilty.

Bullies Need Guardian Angels, Too

Ernest P. Higgs was in the top form of Maryfield Primary School. He was eleven years old, the biggest boy in the school. His father owned the biggest car, wore a gold chain round his neck and his mother wore the brightest and most expensive clothes and always wore the biggest hats as if she was going to a wedding or to see the Queen.

Ernest – everyone called him Ernie – always wore the most expensive trainers, his pockets were always full of sweets and he owned the most expensive mobile phone you could imagine, which, despite the school rules to the contrary, he managed to hide in his trouser pocket.

He was also a bully. And most of the other children were afraid of him. All except Daniel (and we shall hear about him later.) It wasn't as if Ernie was mean. Far from it. He handed out sweets to everyone, was generous with his money and always offered to give lifts home in his father's Rolls Royce. He gave the most exciting birthday parties and, on bonfire night, his fireworks were bigger and brighter than anyone else's. At Christmas, his father dressed up as Father Christmas and handed out very expensive presents to all the children in the school. But no-one liked him. Everyone was afraid of Ernie, except for two boys from the class below him who ate his sweets and told him how brave he was, how clever and how everyone else was stupid and cowardly. Ernie called these boys his bodyguards and, sometimes, his slaves, and ordered them around as if he was the King of the Castle.

Ernie was also tall and handsome with lots of curly black hair and a round smiley face. He liked games, although he turned nasty if his side wasn't winning, and he called the boys on the other side rude names. Once, he was sent off the pitch for deliberately tripping up a player from a visiting team. The girls liked him at first because he gave them little presents such as rings and bracelets which his father gave him from one of his shops. It was always the same story. At first, the girl would laugh and joke with him and then Ernie couldn't resist bullying her. He would call her insulting names like Spotty face or Snakey hair or Cheesey feet, and other rude names as well. Then the girl would burst into tears and run off to tell the teacher and Ernie would be summoned to Mr Livingstone in the Head teacher's study and given a good telling off. But nothing anyone said or did could change Ernie. They didn't have to put up with him much longer, however. At the end of term Ernie would leave Maryfield

School and next term he would go to his big expensive private school which he was always boasting about. Meanwhile, they all had to put up with Ernie's bullying. He was always picking fights with the other boys and his bodyguards were always there by his side ready to defend him. Ernie never started a fight unless his body guards were with him.

But Daniel was different. Daniel was also in the top form and he lived with his mother in his grandmother's house because his father had gone off to work one day and had never come home again. At first, Daniel missed his father, but, as time passed, he settled down to life with his mother and granny and was happy. His mother went out to work looking after ill people, but his granny always met him after school and drove him home in her little car.

He was going to be eleven soon and granny said he could have a party in her garden and her friend, Thomas, would come along and cook hot dogs and hamburgers on the barbecue. Daniel was popular and granny said he could invite anyone he liked. Daniel was told to write out the invitations telling the guests what time to come to the party and where it was to be held. It was an exciting time!

Daniel was a bright boy, not particularly tall, but

sturdily built, good at football where he ran rings round Ernie who blundered about like a water buffalo. Daniel had a cheerful face, short brown hair and lovely brown eyes that seemed to twinkle away with secret jokes. He had no enemies, lots of friends and he kept well away from Ernie.

Now Ernie really disliked Daniel (he was jealous of him, of course), but however hard he tried, he couldn't pick a fight with Daniel and he couldn't beat him at anything. Ernie, however, really wanted to go to Daniel's birthday party. Everyone else in the top class had been invited, but not Ernie. He would do anything to get one of those invitations. He even offered Daniel a whole bag of Liquorice Allsorts and said his dad would drive him home in his Rolls Royce. But Daniel only laughed and said he didn't like Liquorice Allsorts and his granny always came in her car to take him home.

It was granny who came to Ernie's rescue. She saw him talking to Daniel and she wound down her car window and watched them. She saw Ernie offer Daniel some sweets, saw Daniel shake his head and saw Ernie's sad face. She saw him rub his eyes with the sleeve of his jacket and realised that Ernie, the Great Ernie, was actually crying.

'What's the matter with Ernie?' said granny as Daniel ran up to the car and opened the door of the back seat.

'He wants to come to my party. He'll only cause trouble.'

'Hmm –' said granny, as she started up the engine. 'He could help Thomas with the barbecue, and, besides,' she said with a little smile, 'he'll give you a wopping big present, that's for sure. Bigger than all the others put together, I should think.'

'I'll think about it,' said Daniel getting into the car, 'I suppose he can't do any harm if we're all there.'

'Course not,' said granny as she drove off, 'Thomas won't stand for any trouble. Ernie'll behave himself, you'll see.'

Well, Ernie got his invitation and Daniel got his big present – a table top football game with two teams, one with red shirts and the other in blue shirts. It fitted perfectly on one of granny's large garden tables and was very popular with all Daniel's friends.

Thomas cooked the sausages and Ernie ate four hot dogs and said he felt sick.

'You need to run around a bit,' said granny. 'What about a game of hide and seek? Come on Ernie, you start us off. You go and hide somewhere, we'll count to a

hundred and then come and find you.'

So Ernie lumbered off looking for somewhere to hide and Daniel tried not to see where he was going.

At the far end of the garden was a wooden shed. It had been there for years and years and was full of junk. Granny was always saying she was going to clear it out but she never got round to it.

Ernie spotted the shed. The key was on the outside of the lock and he opened the door and went inside. It was stuffed full of junk and an old wooden cupboard blocked the only window, so when he shut the door, it was almost dark. He retreated behind and old lawn mower and crouched down and waited.

Daniel had seen where Ernie was heading and guessed where he was hiding. As soon as granny gave the signal to start looking, Daniel made for the shed. The others were all hunting around in the shrubbery and took no notice of him. Then Daniel had a wicked idea. He crept forward and locked the shed door. With a little smile, Daniel ran back to join the others.

Inside the shed, Ernie began to feel a bit scared. It was gloomy and there were lots of cobwebs around, hanging from the cupboards and piles of boxes. Ernie knew that where there were cobwebs there were SPIDERS! Now Ernie hated spiders. In fact, he was terrified of spiders. He decided it was time to give himself up and get out of that horrid shed. He stood up, pushed aside a big box that was blocking his way and made for the door. Then he saw it! It was the biggest, fattest, blackest spider he'd ever seen. It had eight very long hairy legs and sat there looking at Ernie. It was, in fact, more frightened of Ernie than Ernie was of him, but Ernie didn't stop to think about that. He gave a great bellow of fear and ran towards the door. He tried to open it, but found someone had locked it and now he couldn't get out and he felt sure the spider was coming after him. He screamed and shouted to be let out. He banged on the door. No-one heard him. He felt certain that this was going to be the end of Ernie P. Higgs.

Just then, Daniel's mother came home from work. There had been an emergency and she had asked granny and Thomas to get the party going and she would join in when she could. She helped herself to a hamburger and passed granny a cup of tea.

'I am sure you could do with this,' she said. 'Thanks for your help. By the way, where's that bully boy Ernie? His parents are coming any minute with a great bag of fireworks.'

'We can't find him,' said Jenny, one of the guests. 'He's hiding somewhere.'

'Really? I would think he would want to help finish off these hamburgers. Hallo? What's that noise I can hear? Someone shouting… Daniel, what have you done?' said mother suddenly noticing Daniel's red face.

'It's nothing,' Daniel stammered. 'Just some work-men.'

'Workmen? Can't be. Since when did workmen go around hammering and banging on a Saturday afternoon? Daniel, why are you looking guilty? You haven't...?

'I only wanted to teach him a lesson. He's always winding me up,' said Daniel.

But mother was off, followed by all the children. They ran to the shed and unlocked the door and Ernie fell out.

'Please, please, don't let him get me,' he sobbed.

'Who?' said mother, helping Ernie up and putting her arms round his trembling shoulders.

'The spider. A huge, hairy spider; as big as a dinner plate.'

'I don't think so,' said mother as all the children gasped and backed away from the open door. 'Let's have a look.'

She peered inside and couldn't see very much, only a tiddly little spider sitting on top of one of the boxes.

'He's just a baby and probably terrified of you. Now come along and have a hamburger and let's see if your dad has come with the fireworks. He's going to need your help, I should think. Oh yes, I've brought along a

chocolate cake for pudding and we want you to show us how to play football with that wonderful present you've given Daniel.'

'Seems you were Ernie's guardian angel, Sally,' said granny when they had all gone back to the house. 'And, Daniel, that was a very bad thing you did. Ernie was really frightened of that spider and he is one of your guests and you should've looked after him. I think you owe him an apology.'

Well, after a while, Ernie began to enjoy himself and he loved helping his father set off the fireworks. He soon forgot all about the spider and quickly forgave Daniel.

When the party was over, Ernie's father gave all the children a long ride in his car and everyone agreed it had been the best birthday party ever.

Granny took Daniel aside, after everyone had gone home, and whispered to him, 'You see, Daniel, even bullies need guardian angels sometimes. This time it was your mother who saved him.'

Watch Out For The Red Flags

Malus Maximus, otherwise known as Old Maxie, the enemy of The Holy One and his angels, woke up feeling very grumpy. He glared round his cave and saw most of his demons fast asleep on the sandy floor. Others were quietly playing cards and stuffing themselves with bacon sandwiches (their favourite) and drinking goblets of Maxie's own beer.

The cheek of it, he thought, and he felt his temper surge up inside him. When his temper flared up like this, smoke came out of his nostrils, and when he got even more angry, sparks flew out followed by flames. He

uncoiled himself and stared with his bloodshot eyes at the peaceful scene. Then he let out a gigantic bellow that made all the little demons jump in fright.

'Come here, you idle lay-abouts, you slackers and gluttons! Where's Shifty and Sneaker? It's time for action, not idleness.'

Now Shifty and Sneaker were two of the pig-like demons, a bit bigger than the others, with large, rather friendly faces. They were Maxie's spies, good at changing their shape into angels and able to live up on one of the heavenly clouds with the other angels and watch and listen to everything that was going on.

'Well, you two,' roared Maxie, as the two demons came running forward. 'What have you to report today? How is it with our Enemy? Or, perhaps you have decided to change sides? Better grub up there, I suppose? Lots more beer?'

'Oh no, Great Lord,' said Sneaker. 'We would never do that. We promised to serve you for all time. We would never join up with those boring angels.'

'Well, come here and tell us what you've heard. And you, lazy bunch of useless servants, come and listen to what Sneaker and Shifty have to say.'

All the pig-demons came rushing up to Maxie and

pushed and shoved each other for the best places. Some jumped up on Maxie's scaly back and gently scratched him behind his tiny, crocodile ears. This always calmed him down.

'The angels are happy,' began Sneaker. 'Their boss is pleased with them because they have defeated us several times now. They are always playing on their musical instruments and singing their stupid songs and eating that disgusting honey of theirs.'

'So, our Enemy thinks he is winning our eternal battle. He thinks he is victorious, I suppose. Well, we'll have to change all that, won't we?' said Maxie, glaring ominously at his anxious servants.

'Yes, Great Lord,' they chanted. 'It's time for action.'

'Then, sound the trumpets, beat the drums, tell the world that Old Maxie is not dead, neither has he given up. We shall defeat our Enemy, yet.'

The demons ran to fetch their instruments and for a few minutes the cave shook with the noise from the trumpets, a harsh blaring sound, and the beating of the drums. After a while, Old Maxie told them to stop.

'That's enough. Now, tell us where does our Enemy think he has gained this so-called victory?'

'There is a place in England called Maryfield. Each

time we try to tempt those children to do bad things, Stevie and that friend of his Angelina, interfere and stop us,' said Sneaker.

'Then we must go back to this place, Maryfield, and try again. What's the name of that boy who tried to hurt our friend, Ernie?'

'He's called Daniel,' said Sneaker. 'A tiresome child, but clever. He deserves to be punished.'

'Well, let's start with him,' said Old Maxie. 'Now, let's fill up our goblets and drink to the downfall of our Enemy. Pincher and Poker, fetch the beer and see that everyone drinks his fill.'

Well, how happy the demons were! They were going to have a party. They danced round Old Maxie singing his praises and holding out their goblets for more beer. As for the old dragon, he coiled himself up again and lay there basking in the attentions of his servants. He knew them all so well. Give them plenty to eat and plenty to drink, and they would do anything for him. That Daniel, he thought, didn't stand a chance!

And so the party went on all night and all the next day whilst Malus Maximus waited his chance.

It was half term and the weather had turned very hot.

Daniel's granny came up with a bright idea. As Daniel's mother was working, she said she would drive Daniel down to the sea-side where her friend, Thomas, owned a beach hut. Daniel had been there several times before and he always loved going there. He also liked Thomas who was quite old, but liked all things connected with the sea, such as sailing boats, rowing canoes, collecting shells and swimming in the sea. He also liked eating ice-creams.

Thomas said he would cook sausages and granny made some ginger bread men and packed up some cheese sandwiches and apples and bananas.

They set off early in granny's little yellow car and drove towards the big town of Brighton. Just before they reached the town, they turned off towards the coast. There, they could park their car and Daniel helped granny carry the bag of food over to the Promenade. There was Thomas waiting for them at the top of the steps. He was dressed in an old blue and white striped shirt and baggy shorts and his feet were bare. He was so pleased to see them and took the bag of food and led the way to the beach hut. It was just marvellous! Thomas had painted the hut bright blue and it had a yellow door with the number 205 painted on it with black paint. That

89

morning the door was wide open, so if the sun was too strong, they could all sit inside it.

Daniel looked out towards the sea which had receded from the Promenade leaving behind a lovely stretch of sand. The sun was shining, there was just a light breeze to keep them cool and the conditions were perfect for swimming. It didn't take them long to unpack the food, put on their swimming costumes, and make for the beach. On the way to the sea, they stopped to talk to the two life guards who were chatting to their friends.

'Watch out for the red flag,' said one of the life guards who was called Patrick, Pat to his friends. The weather will start blowing a gale later today and the sea will get too rough for swimming. It's all right now, but see those big clouds up there? Well, they'll get bigger later on and then we'll have rain as well as wind. Better get your swimming over and done with now, whilst the sea's calm. When the red flag is flying, then definitely no swimming. Just remember to look out for it.'

After they had had a wonderful time in the sea and had wandered up to the Promenade, collecting shells on their way and waving to friends, they returned to the beach hut, where Thomas cooked sausages on a small camping barbecue and granny unpacked the ginger bread and sandwiches. Other people from the neighbouring huts came to talk to them and time passed very quickly. When they were once more on their own, granny packed away the remains of the picnic and announced that she and Thomas wanted to have a short nap before she drove home. She promised that, when she woke up, she would treat Daniel and Thomas to ice-creams from the Italian cafe further along the Promenade. Thomas was quite happy sorting out the shells and playing computer games. Soon, granny and Thomas were fast asleep in their beach chairs.

Daniel hadn't noticed that the tide had come in whilst they had all been occupied with their friends and the picnic. Also, the wind was now blowing a bit harder. Daniel became bored with sitting still and he looked round to see if there were any children around who would like to play football with him on the strip of grass around the Putting Green which was on the other side of the Promenade, near the coast road. There was no one around. It was very quiet except for the surging of the sea as the waves came crashing up the beach towards the Promenade.

Suddenly, Daniel had an idea. He always loved the big waves, feeling the power of the tide and jumping high up in the air to get above the waves and then swimming with them towards the shore. He looked round to check that granny and Thomas were still asleep in their comfortable chairs and Pat, the life guard seemed to be asleep further along the Promenade. He felt alone and brave and ready for an adventure. He didn't notice the red flag flying from its pole further along the Promenade.

He pulled off his T shirt and walked quickly towards the steps leading down to the beach. The sea had come in fast now and the sandy beach had disappeared and the big waves were now crashing against the Promenade. Wonderful! The sun had disappeared behind a thick layer of cloud and the wind was roaring around like an angry lion released from its cage. The beach had changed from being a friendly, welcoming place to a place of danger and darkness – and adventure!

Daniel liked the feeling of being just a little bit frightened. He knew he was a good swimmer and was the fastest swimmer in his school at the local Leisure Centre swimming pool. But this wasn't the Leisure Centre!

He went to the top of the steps and waited for a wave to come surging towards him. Soon, a big one came towards him and then he jumped off the steps and into the sea. The wave retreated and the next one came along and swept Daniel away from the steps and out into the sea. Oh, the excitement of feeling the surge of the water, and the power of the retreating tide.

The next wave came hurtling towards him, the spray dashing against his face. He swallowed a great mouthful of sea water and began to feel just a little bit afraid. This was too much of an adventure. It wasn't fun any more.

He was soon tired and tried to put his feet down on the beach when the wave retreated. For a second, he felt the gravel under his toes and then a powerful force dragged him out into the sea again. It was a force so powerful that he couldn't stand up against it. He remembered then that granny had warned him against this force which she called the undertow and she had said that it was very dangerous indeed. As the tide retreated, then the force would increase.

Well, Daniel began to feel very frightened indeed. He couldn't stand up, he couldn't swim back to the steps and gradually, very gradually, he felt as if he was being dragged out to sea. The sea had got him in its clutches and would not let him go. He looked towards the Promenade where granny and Thomas were still fast asleep, but the coast seemed to be getting further and further away. To make matters worse, the rain had come, just as Pat had forecast, and was beating down on his head.

He tried to call out Help! But a wave came and hit him in the face. He was terrified. No-one could hear him. No-one had seen him.

Then, just as Daniel felt his strength ebbing away, he heard the roar of a powerful engine. It was more powerful than the sound of the wind and the crashing of the waves. Just as another wave burst over him, making him gasp for breath, he saw it. It was a bright blue and orange motor boat coming from the direction of Shoreham, the next port along the coast, and heading towards him. The spray was crashing over its bow and the life boat crew were shouting and waving to him. It was the RNLI rescue boat. Pat had summoned it from Shoreham with his mobile phone as soon as he saw Daniel leap into the sea. Even though Pat was a strong swimmer, he was not strong enough to swim against the force of the waves and tide.

The boat surged towards Daniel, and someone threw him a bright orange ring which he clutched hold of and gradually felt himself drawn to the side of an orange dinghy which had been lowered from the life boat and would bring him to the shore. He was safe! But only just in time.

No-one told him off that day. He was too weak to do anything and had to go to the local hospital to be checked over. Later, however, when granny and Thomas came to take him home. Thomas looked at him sternly.

'Didn't you see the Red Flag?'

'I forgot to look.'

'You must always look before you go into the sea. Didn't Pat tell you not to swim when the flag was flying? We have had one of the worst storms of the year and there you were trying to take a swim. Pat is very upset that he didn't notice you going to the steps. He had closed his eyes for a few seconds and that was the time you jumped into the sea.'

'He saw me later, though,' whispered Daniel.

'He did indeed and the life boat came to your rescue. Your guardian angels were out in force today, I think. I'll take you to meet the RNLI – the Royal Life Boat Institution, it's called – when you are fully recovered.'

Once again, Old Maxie was out-witted. Will he try again, do you think?

Summer Fair

Stevie looked up at the great angel Michael, who was sitting on his cloud, his huge wings folded away, a look of concern on his face. Stevie felt just a little bit anxious. It wasn't usual for Michael to summon one of the lesser angels to his special cloud. What had he done? Stevie thought. He wished Angelina was with him to hold his hand, but Michael had asked to see him alone on an important matter.

Michael noticed Stevie's reluctance to come forward.

'Come up here, Stevie,' he said kindly, patting the cloud beside him.

'Don't be anxious. You've not done anything wrong. It's just something I've heard which I would like to discuss with you.'

He smiled and his face glowed with a radiant light. Stevie breathed a sigh of relief. He climbed up onto Michael's cloud and sat down, cross-legged, next to Michael.

'What's up, Sir?' said Stevie.

'Well, I've heard from two of my informants – spies, I suppose you'd call them – that our Enemy, that old dragon who calls himself Malus Maximus…'

'You mean Old Maxie?' said Stevie.

Michael laughed. 'That's the one. Well, two of his spies also work for us, the servants of The Holy One.'

'You mean they are double agents?' said Stevie importantly.

'That's right. I don't trust them, of course, but they have their uses. Well, it seems Old Maxie is about to launch a major attack on us. He's furious at the way we keep interfering with his evil plans. He was particularly angry when we shut Ernie, one of his promising recruits, in that shed with that spider and you saved Daniel that day when he was nearly drowned in the sea.'

'I only jogged Pat, the life-guard, and he did the rest.'

Absolutely, but you saved Daniel's life. And now, Old Maxie's out for revenge. He's targeting Maryfield, the school in particular, so you must be alert. I'll get you some help as I expect you will need reinforcements.'

'I'll get down there right away,' said Stevie, jumping up. 'I wonder when the old rascal will attack and how.'

'I'll let you know more when I've spoken to the spies. They might be persuaded to spill a few more beans.'

'Who are they, by the way?' said Stevie, wondering if they were special friends of his.

'I think they are called Shifty and Sneaker when they

are working for Old Maxie. I call them Judas 1 and Judas 2 and I don't think you know them. They don't mix much with the angels but they are quite happy to report what's going on in Maxie's camp and I pay them in our own special Angel cakes, which they love. Don't give them another thought because they are poor, sad creatures serving two masters.'

Stevie didn't know anyone called Judas 1 and Judas 2 so he bowed to Michael and flew off to alert Angelina. There was trouble coming!

Only a few more days and then it would be the end of term; and that meant that it was time for the Summer Fair.

This was always a big event with lots of stalls and games and ice-creams and ladies painting children's faces. This year was going to be special. A local band was coming to play to them and Mr Livingstone, the headmaster, with the help of parents, had built a stage for the band at one end of the field. This stage was rather grand with an archway at one end. This had been constructed from runner bean poles and was decorated with coloured lights which were going to wink on and off throughout the afternoon. The stage was a bit wobbly, though, but that didn't matter, said Mr Livingstone, as long as the band didn't jump up and down too much.

The day of the Fair was sunny and warm and Daniel was up early helping his granny and his mother, who had the day off, carry the trays of cakes and scones which they had made to one of the tables which was to be the cake stall. In the centre of the table granny had carefully placed a beautiful birthday cake, because that day was her friend Thomas's birthday. Daniel didn't know how old Thomas was and granny had only put eight candles on the cake and Daniel Knew that, of course, Thomas couldn't be only eight years old. That was stupid. But granny had said, winking at him, if she put the real number of candles on the cake it would not be big enough for them. Thomas was going to cut the cake later in the afternoon and sell slices of it for one pound a slice.

There was a plant stall next to the cake stall and a Tombola stall and a table with all the raffle prizes on it. Someone was selling balloons and lots of the children had bought them and were dashing around hitting each other to see how many hits were needed to burst the balloons. It was a wonderful sight and everyone was cheerful and happy to spend money which was to go to Maryfield school.

Then the band arrived at three o'clock and the musicians, there were four of them, began to tune up their guitars and set up the drums. Mr and Mrs Fairbrother, who were running the tea stall, soon became very busy selling cups of tea and people were rushing to buy ice-creams from the ice-cream van which had just arrived. Granny's stall soon sold out of cakes and scones and she was beginning to wish she'd baked more. The birthday cake was still there, though, and Thomas was going to cut it at half past three. What a lot of money they were going to make, said Mr Livingstone to the plant stall lady. Nothing could go wrong. Could it? Of course not.

But...

Next to the School field, usually the playing field where the children played football and had held their Sports Day, was another field separated from the School field by a big hedge and a five-barred gate. This field belonged to a local farmer, a Mr Percy Hopkins, who sometimes used it for grazing for his three donkeys who used to stand hopefully at the gate waiting for the children to come and talk to them. They were family pets and everyone made a fuss of them.

That afternoon, Percy Hopkins had put twelve bullocks in that field so that they could enjoy a bit of freedom. These bullocks were young bulls, not quite grown up, like teenager bulls. Twelve lively, dark brown bullocks with curly hair on the top of their heads, had stood on the other side of the gate watching the events going on the field next to them. They found it very exciting and grew even more excited when the band started playing and the children started dashing around with their balloons. Percy Hopkins had forgotten all about the Summer Fair. Besides, what did it matter; the big gate was firmly shut.

Soon, the bullocks were all jostling one another to get a better view through the bars of the gate and began to make bellowing noises. No-one took any notice of them. No-one, except Ernie Higgs, the big bully, who had got over his fright with the spider, had eaten two ice-creams and was getting bored. No-one wanted to talk to him and he was trying to think of a way of getting his own back on Daniel, who had locked him in that shed.

Erne saw his mother and father were busy talking to Mr Livingstone, so he decided to walk over to the gate and talk to the bullocks who were pushing at the gate determined to join in the fun.

No-one saw him walk over to the gate. Certainly, no-one saw him tug back the bolt on the gate. Just a few seconds more to open the gate, just a tiny bit. Then, Whoosh! Twelve, cheerful, over-excited young bullocks charged into the school field and made for the cake stall. They pushed past Ernie, who fell over and nearly got trampled on. He shouted for help for help and this made them even more excited. Thomas saw what had happened and grabbed his cake. Just in time, as the bullocks knocked over the table and sent Daniel's mother and granny running away towards the school house.

Onwards rushed the gang, straight to the plant stall. This was interesting and some of the bullocks made a grab for the plants and sent the table flying. People started screaming and began to chase the bullocks. Someone flapped a tea towel at them. A balloon burst, then another. The band began to play a bit louder. All this only made the gang more excited. Whoosh! Over went the table where the lady was painting the faces of some of the children. Paint pots were trampled on and the children ran off screaming with fright, back to find their parents.

And then the bullocks saw the stage!

The biggest and bravest of the bullocks got to the stage first and butted his head against the wobbly platform, making the drummer fall over, followed by all his drums. Butt, butt! Another bullock joined in, and then another, and another. The other three members of the band threw down their instruments and jumped off the stage. More bullocks joined in the game, making the stage rock and roll so much that the flimsy arch with all its fairy lights and garlands of flowers collapsed with a great crash, sending the bullocks flying away in terror and heading towards the tombola stall.

Meanwhile, Mr Livingstone, furious with the disruption, had made an urgent call on his mobile to Percy Hopkins, who, as it happened, was coming along the road outside the school and was planning to pay a visit to the Fair.

'Hold on,' he yelled. 'I'm coming!'

Leaving his tractor parked in the road outside the school, he ran into the school field. He'd brought with him three wooden poles and thrust one at Mr Livingstone, one at Ernie's father and one for himself.

Percy Hopkins, a stout man with a loud voice, yelled instructions at his two assistants, and followed by a whole mob of children, parents and teachers, advanced on the bullocks. With the skill of an experienced sheep dog, Percy directed his army of assistants in rounding up the gang of bullocks and driving them slowly, but surely, back to their own field.

Ernie, in the meanwhile, had got to his feet and was standing by the gate. He felt terrified about what he had done and he knew that his face was very red, a complete give-away.

As the last of the bullocks tore past him into the field,

Percy Hopkins shouted at him.

'You there, you shut the gate. Quick now, before they try again.'

So Erne shut the gate and slammed home the bolt.

But what confusion there was! What chaos! Fortunately, most of the stalls had sold their produce before the bullocks got at them. The band soon recovered and started up again without the archway. And Thomas still had his cake!

It didn''t take long to make fresh pots of tea and the ice-cream man had survived the attack and soon resumed handing round ice-cream cones.

And then everyone began to laugh and laugh and laugh. All except Ernie who had joined his father and mother and hoped no-one would notice him.

But Mr Livingstone had noticed him.

'A word with you, young man,' he said. And Ernie's face became even redder.

Well, to cut a long story short, Ernie's father came to his rescue and promised to pay for all the damage which the bullocks had caused. He even promised to pay for a brand new stage for the band. It was to be a portable one, on wheels, which could be used for all sorts of occasions, indoors and outdoors.

'Just as well you are leaving this school in a few days,' muttered Mr Livingstone, as he readily accepted Ernie's father's offer.

'He's a good boy, really,' said Ernie's mother holding on to her hat which had fallen off in all the excitement.

'Hm!' said Mr Livingstone. 'That's what they all say.'

'Well, that was a near thing,' whispered Stevie to Angelina, later that day.

'We saved the day, though, and the school made a lot of money,' said Angelina who always looked on the bright side of things.

'And the school is going to get a new stage,' said Stevie as an after-thought.

'One thing, Stevie, where was Old Maxie in all this? Not in the bullocks, surely? They only wanted a bit of fun. You can't really blame them, can you?'

'No, of course not. Old Maxie wasn't in the bullocks. He put the idea into Ernie's head to open the gate. Maxie always works in human beings, you see. He tells us to do bad things and some people don't know how to say 'No' to him.'

'And our job is to tell people to stand up to him, I

suppose,' said Angelina, helping herself to another piece of honey cake.

'That's right. That's why we're called Guardian Angels. Hand over those cakes, Angelina. Being a guardian angel always makes me hungry.'

'And sleepy, too,' said Angelina, giving a big yawn and curling up on her bit of the cloud.

108